ROLLER COASTER
Kid's Guide on How to Write Poetry

Written by Cassidy Kao
Illustrated by Cassidy Kao and Jessica Kao

Rollercoaster Copyright © 2014 by Cassidy Kao

All rights reserved. No part of this book may be reproduced in any form whatsoever, by photography or xerography or any other means, by broadcast or transmission, by translation into any kind of language, nor by recording electronically, or otherwise, without permission in writing form the author, except by a reviewer, who may quote brief passages in critical articles of reviews.

Published in the United States of America

First Print October 2014

ISBN-13: 978-1500468842

ISBN-10: 1500468843

Table of Contents

Chapter 1: Getting Started
    It is FUN to write poems!
    What do you need?
Chapter 2: Rhymed Poems
    Couplet
    Tercet
    Quatrain
    Clerihew
    Limerick
    Triolet
    Sonnet
    Simile
    Opposite
    Riddle
Chapter 3: Unrhymed Poems
    Haiku
    Tanka
    Cinquain
    Acrostic
    Concrete
Chapter 4: Either Rhymed or Unrhymed Poems
    Persona
    List
Chapter 5: Cassidy Invention Poems
    Cassilet
    Freestyle
About the Author and Illustrators

Chapter 1   GETTING STARTED

I wanted to write this book when my mom told me that the month of April was the National Poetry month and that I could compose one poem every day to honor the month. We created a "poet-tree" where I would add a poem-leaf everytime I finished a poem. By the end of April, I wrote so many poems and learned so many different types of poem, I thought I would write a book to show other kids how to write poems. I started by picking out poems to put in the book. I also drew some pictures and asked my cousin, Jessica to draw a few too. We edited out the mistakes and talked about the cover. But mostly we had fun!

It's fun to write poems because you can create your own world. Your mind is like a planet. Everyone has their own planet and each planet has citizens, hundred and hundred of citizens. Just imagine that the citizens are words! You can use the inhabitants of your mind to make sentences which make up your imagination! That's imagination working right there.

Grown ups! Don't worry, your kids will learn something from this book. They will learn about many different types of poems. I will explain how to write each type of poem. I'll show them some examples with my own poems. As a bonus, they will also (if they are planning to write a book of their own) learn a way to organize a poem book, such as introduction, rhyming poems, unrhyming poems, and invented poems and about the author and illustrator. Have fun!

Sincerely,

Cassidy Kao

WHAT TOOLS DO YOU NEED TO GET STARTED?

If you are planning to write poems of your own, here is a list of what you need to get started.

Mandatory Tools
- Creativity and Imagination
- Writing tools of your choice
- Paper
- This book

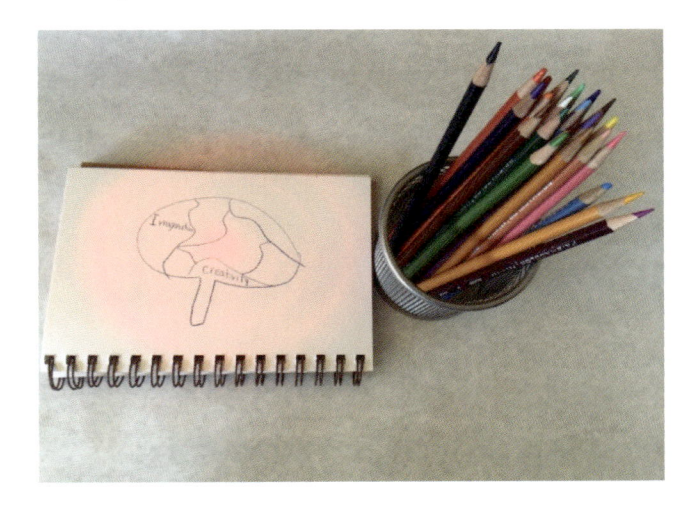

Optional Tools
- Rhyming Dictionary
- Dictionary
- Thesaurus

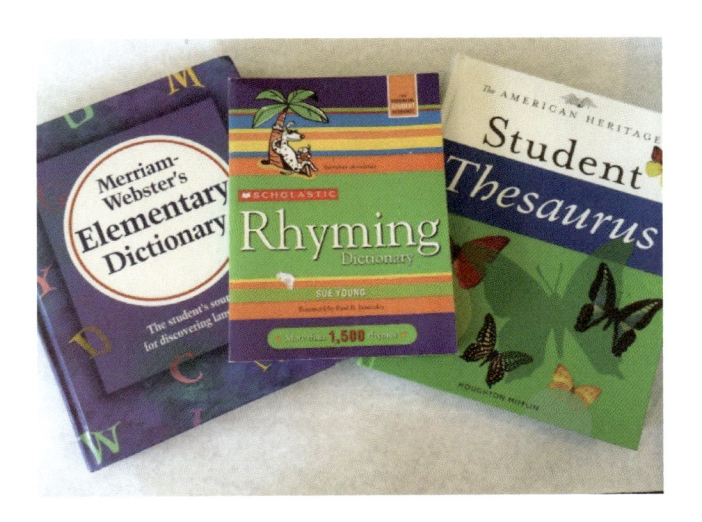

Chapter 2　　RHYMED POEMS

Couplet
To write a couplet, you have to have two lines that rhyme with each other like these poems here:

World of Me

In the world of me
Everyone despises a bee!
(Hee Hee!)

3

Shirt

You never want to get dirt
On your SHIRT!

Tercet
To write a Tercet, you have three lines that all rhyme with each other like these next ones here:

Mixed

I have bones
But I don't own a phony phone
I just want an ice cream cone!
(Word!)

Books

Books
Have hooks
And can go on nooks

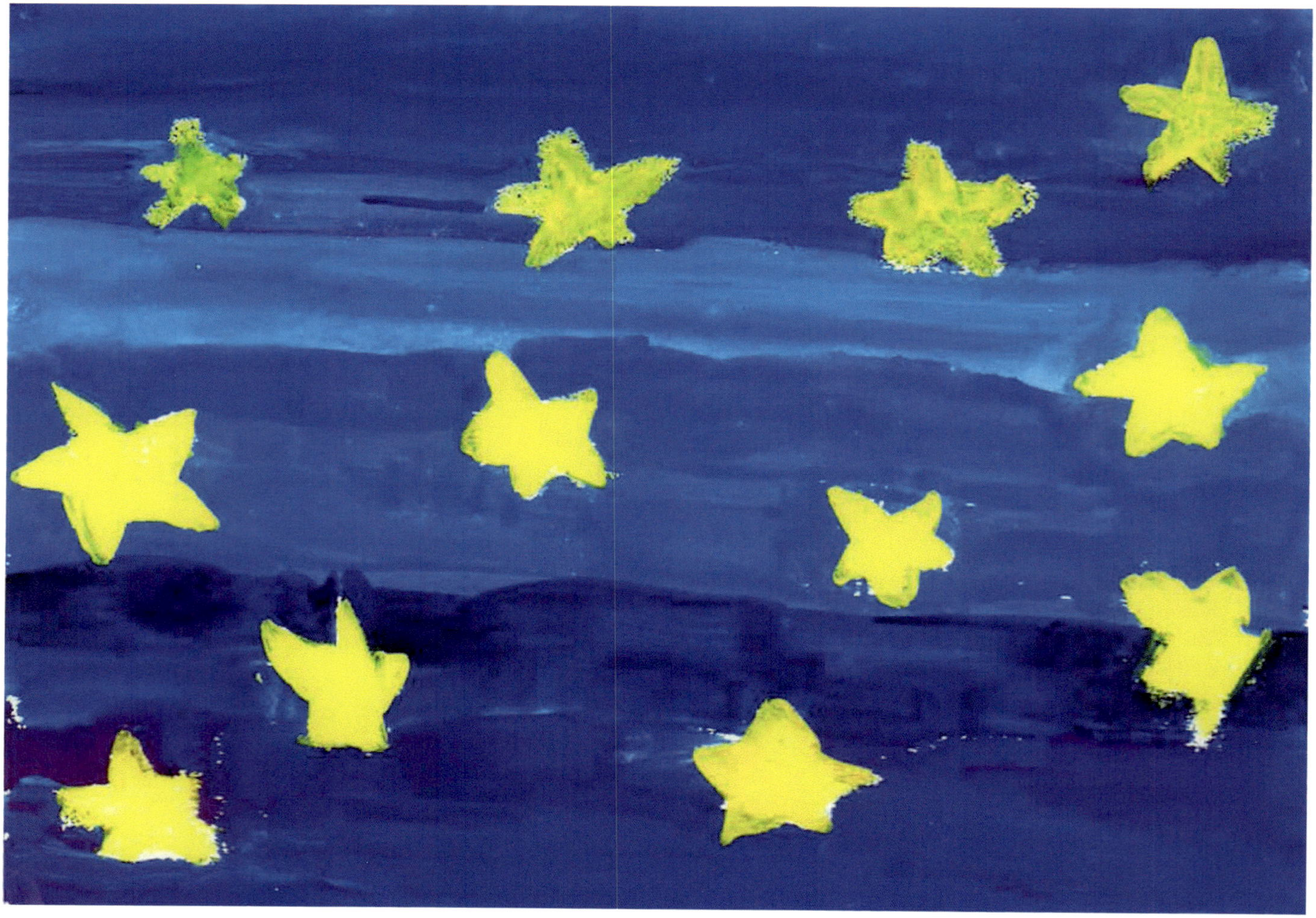

Gravity

If there was no gravity, it would be fun
If there was no gravity, I wouldn't have to run
But, if there was no gravity, there is no 9-1-1

Quatrain

To write a Quatrain, you have four lines with a rhyming sequence of: a-b-a-b or a-a-b-b. You can pick and choose like these ones!

Mr. Curtain

My name is Mr. Curtain
I have a lot of soap
My name always rhymes with Mr. Purtain's
I really love to mope!

10

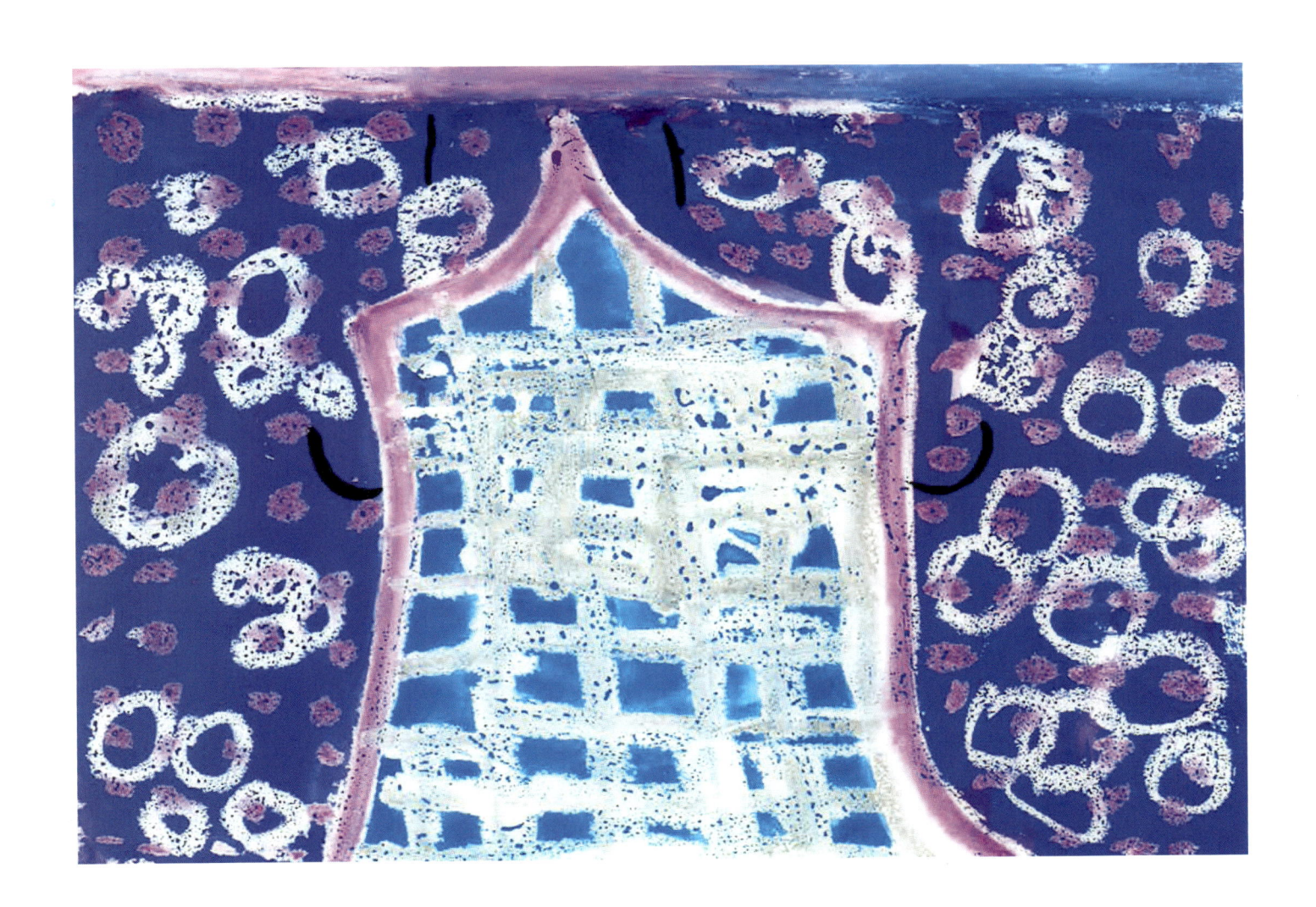

She

She is really nice
She has a bit of lice
She also has some bones
Her head is like a cone!

Sand dollar

Sand dollars are everywhere
Haunting me from here to there
My oh my what can I do
Ah! That one will soooo bite you.

Clerihew

To write a Clerihew (Clery-Hue), you have four lines with the rhyming sequence: a-a-b-b, but the poem has to be humorous and about a famous person or a celebrity and the first line has to be the person's name like this one:

William Shakespeare

William Shakespeare
Drank a lot of beer
And when he sneezed
What always came out was cheese!

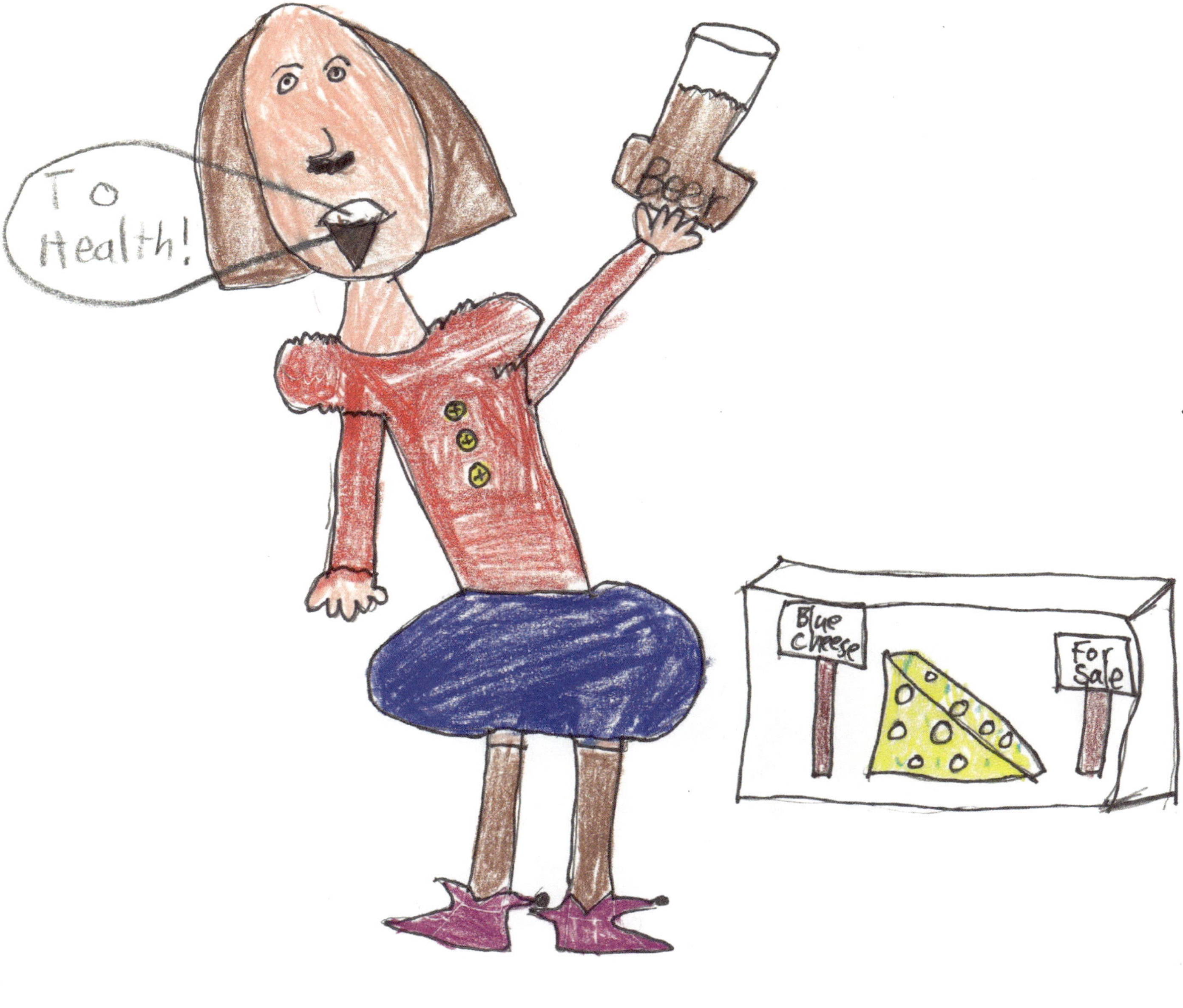
To Health!
Beer
Blue Cheese
For Sale

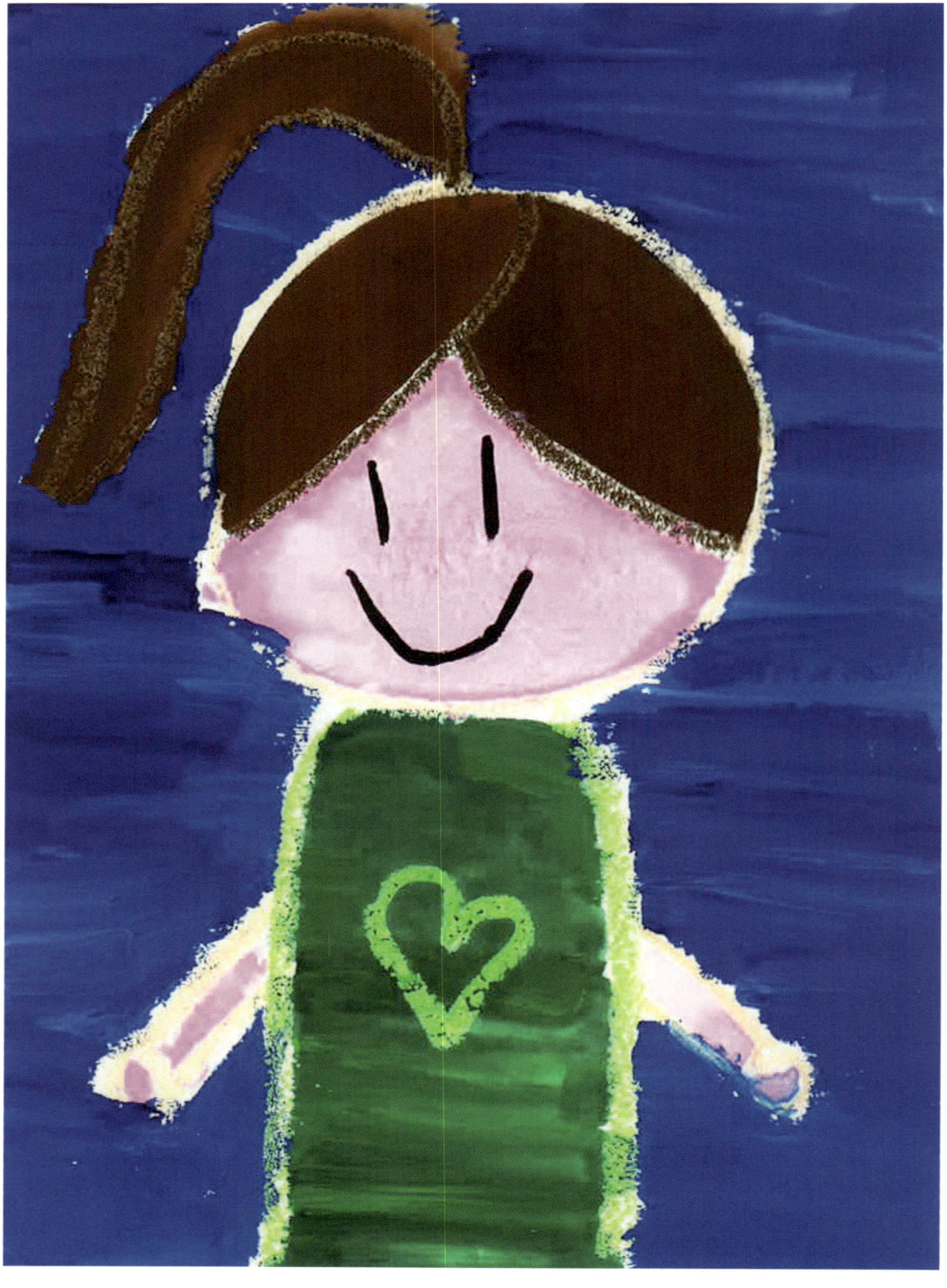

Limerick
To write a Limerick, you must have five lines with a rhyming sequence of a-a-b-b-a and it is usually funny like these ones:

Cassidy

There was a girl named Cassidy
Whose name always rhymed with passidy
She's really allergic to cats
And would never want to see a bat
Oh, the funny Wassidy!

Night

Children of the night
Waiting for a fight
With the sun!
Better run!
For the fight-night!

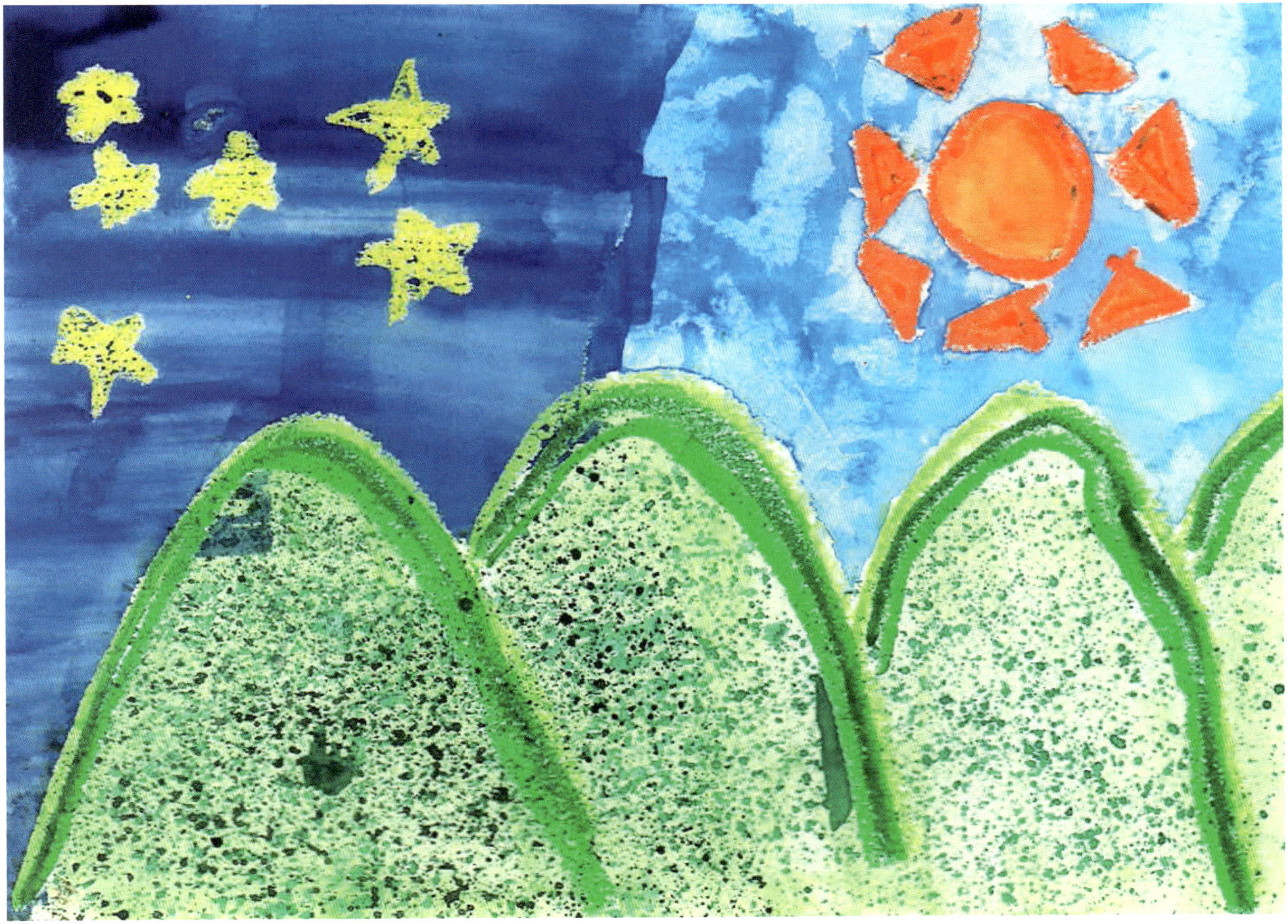

Triolet

To write a Triolet, you must have eight lines that have a rhyming sequence of a-b-a-a-a-b-a-b and line one has to be the same exact words of line 4 and line 7 while line 2 has the exact same words as line 8 like this:

Light

Oh, light is so white and clear
It even makes the rainbow
In a dark room you can use it to peer
Oh, light is so white and clear
So you don't fall and nick your ear
When you sew
Oh, light is so white and clear
It even makes the rainbow

Sonnet

To write a Sonnet, you have to have three quatrains and one couplet at the end. Usually a Shakespearean Sonnet has 10 syllables on each line. My example is a variation that has six syllables on each line.

Flower Sonnet

My oh, my a daisy
Standing in this black haze
Someone must be crazy
To plant this plant un-fazed

My oh, my a lily
Standing in the wild
Someone is knocked silly
Someone is a child

My oh, my a blue star
Standing in this tarred yard
Someone is real bizarre
And think he is a bard

Now you've heard these curses
Bring in the plant nurses

21

Simile

To write a Simile poem, you have as many lines as you like that can have any rhyming sequence but the poem has to have the word "like" in it, like this fine example:

Me

I have black hair
    An intense black stare
        I am like a black cat
    Or a vampire bat
        Ready to come and EAT YOU!

Opposite
To write an Opposite poem, you must have a question (one line) that asks about: what is the opposite of _____? Then a reply that answers the question (another line) like this one:

Us

What is the opposite of us?
Two friends going on another bus.
(*Sigh*)

24

Riddle

To write a riddle poem, you create a riddle that can have as many line as you want but it still has to rhyme like this one:

The Soul

I am the soul some people say
But going home I hurt the whole way
What am I?

(a sole of a shoe)

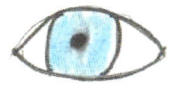

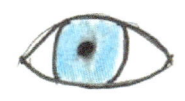

Blind

and yet POOR

Eyes

What has four eyes
But cannot see
A lot of money
But cannot pay the fee?

(Mississippi)

Chapter 3   UNRHYMED POEMS

Haiku

To write a Haiku poem, you have to have three lines that don't rhyme. It has a total of 17 syllables in the poem. Its syllables in the lines are like this: 5-7-5, like the next ones here:

Tree

Trees, Lamb's ear on branch
    Really soft, but really plain
        "Leaves blowing at ease!"

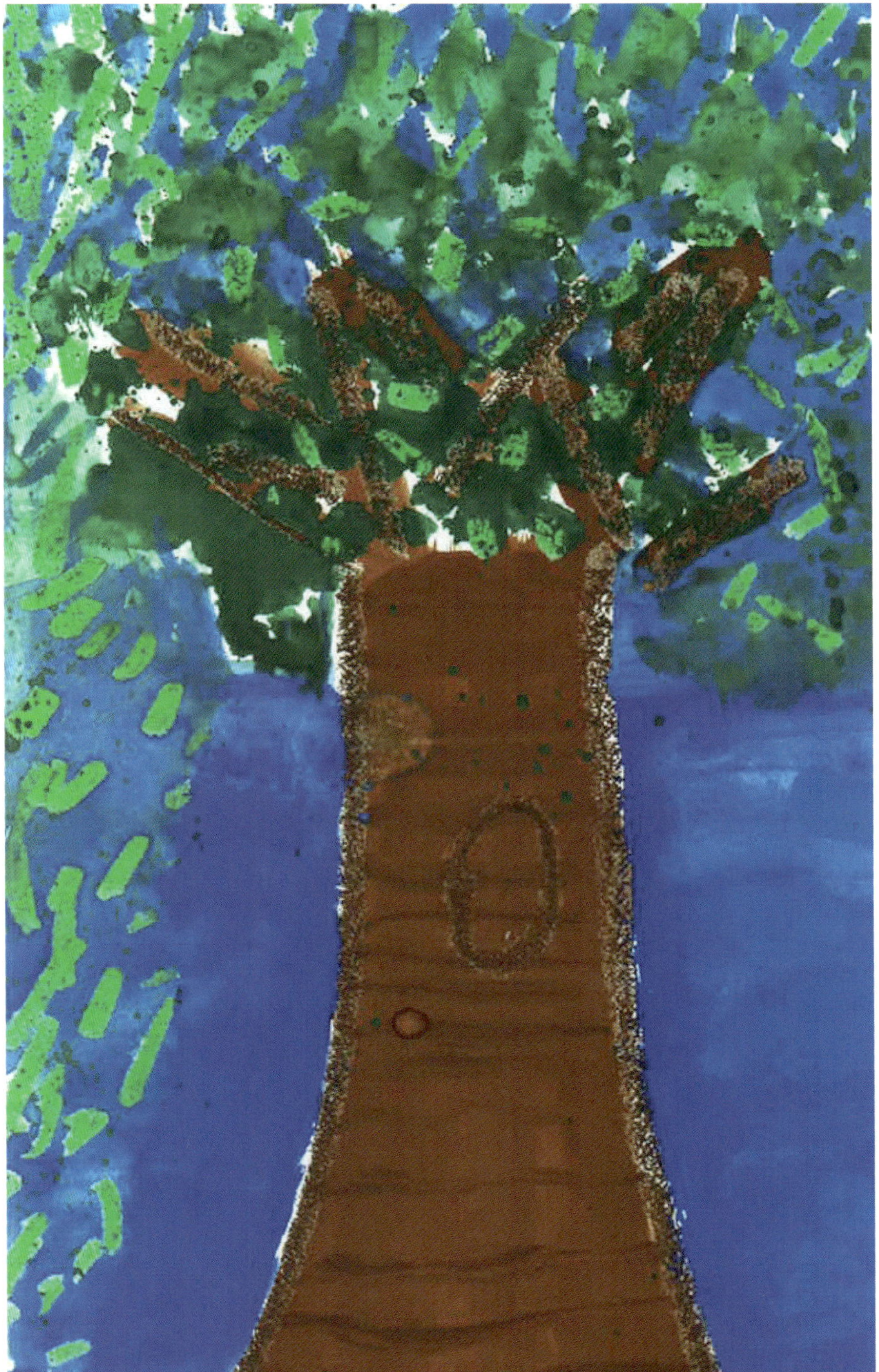

Lizard Sneaks

Lizards are plenty
I know that because I've seen
Many of those sneaks!

Whoosh!

Dog

Dog comes out early
Finds a good place to go bark
Arf! Feels much better.

Houses

There are two houses
One your death, one peace and joy
Reader, do… I…. Lie?

Is this true?

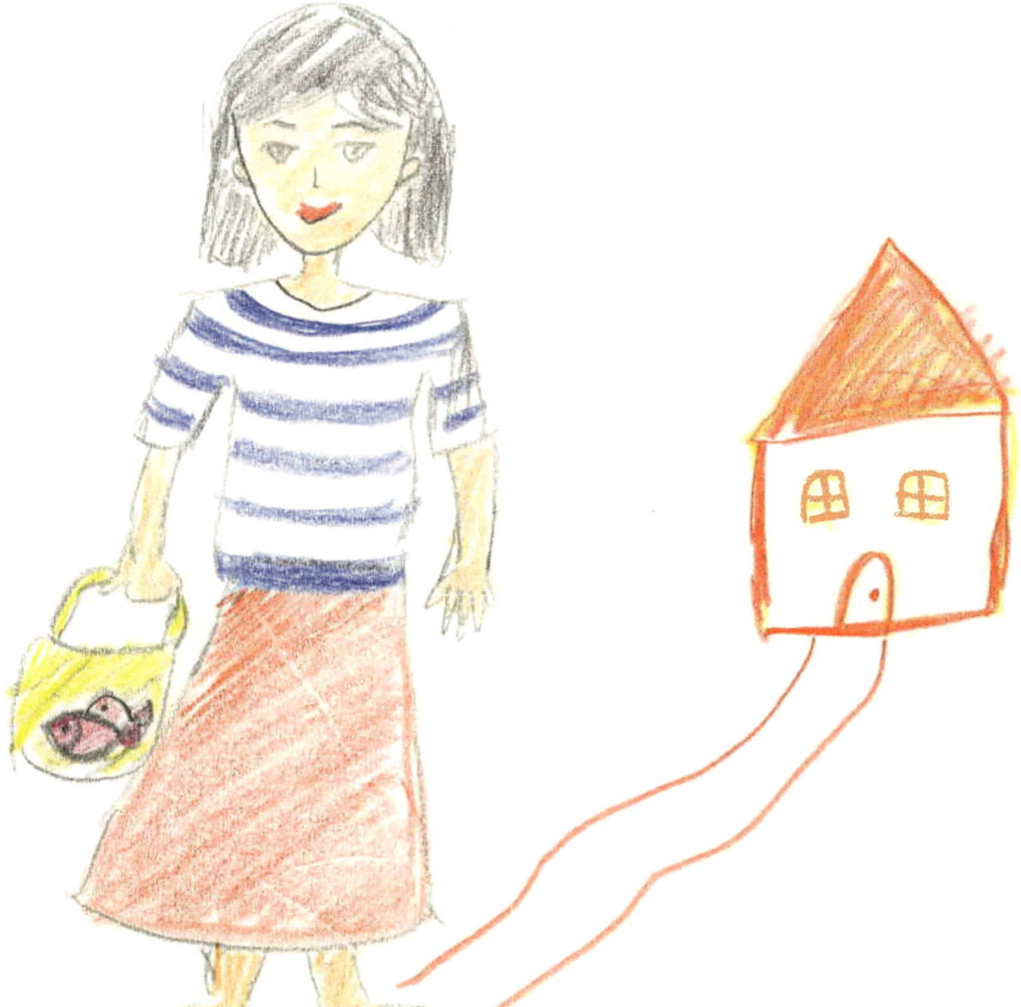

Tanka

To write a Tanka poem, you have five lines that don't rhyme, but it has a special number of syllables on each line: 2-3-2-3-3. You can see an example in the next one:

Mommy buys fish

Mommy
Goes Shopping
Buys fish
Comes right back
Before dark

(a true story)

Cinquain
To write a Cinquain poem, you must have five lines that do not rhyme, and the syllable numbers are: 2-4-6-8-2 like this:

Oh, you

Oh, you
You just standing
around for fun? Oh you
Why do you stand there in the gloom?

Oh You!

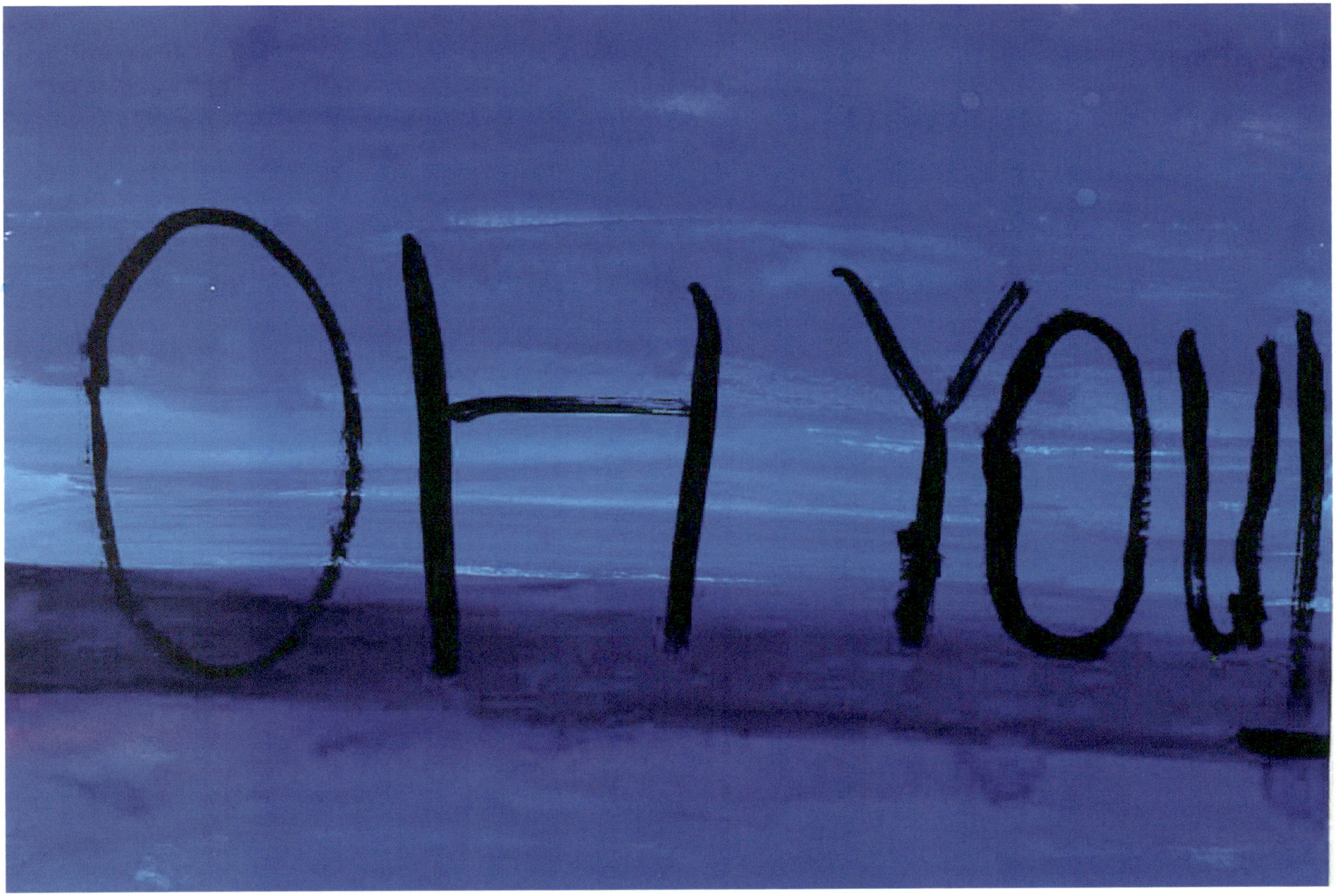
OH YOU

Acrostic

In an acrostic poem, you take the title and spell it vertically. Each letter of the title should serve as the first letter of each line like this:

Sheep

Sits
Hard for
Eons and
Eons. It's now
Parched.

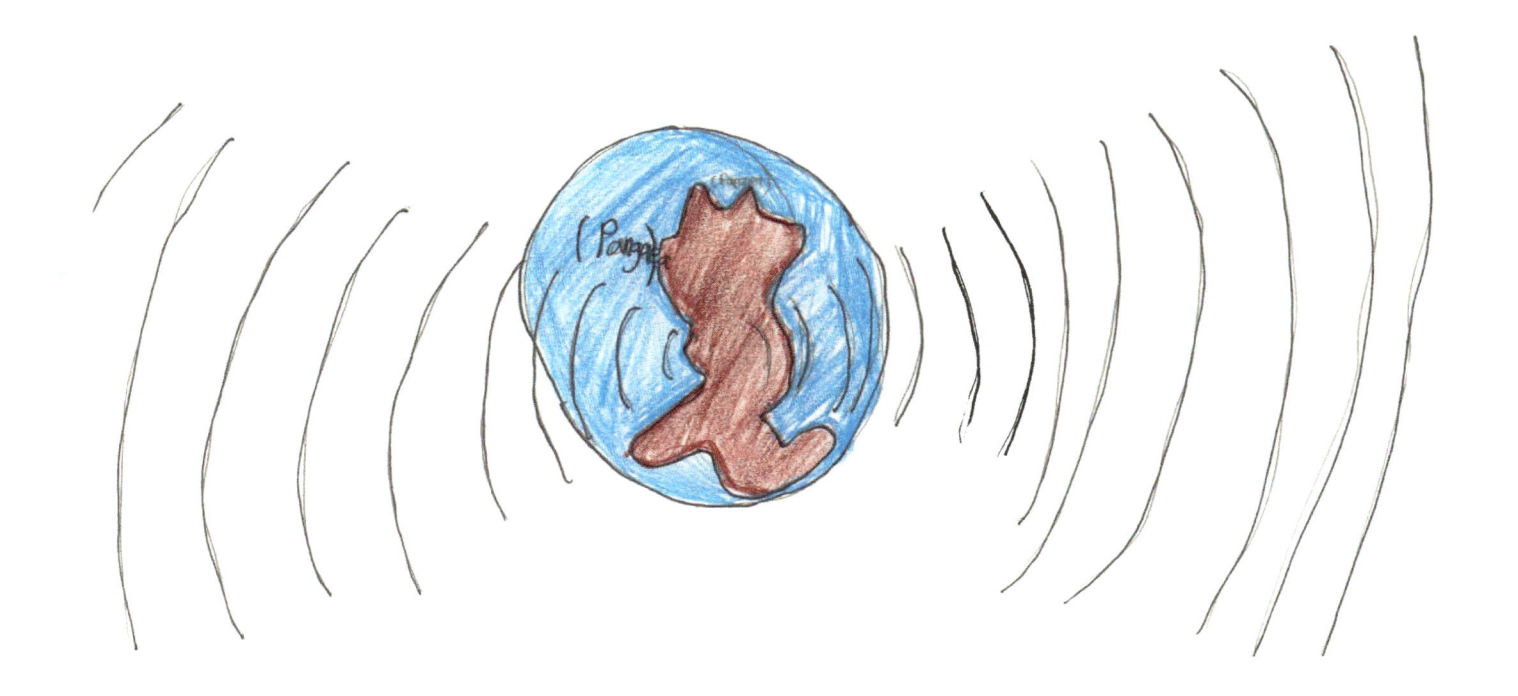

Sound

Sulks
Out of the
Universe and
Never
Die

Daddy

Dogs
                Are
                              Dynamite
                                            Dopes,

        Yes?

Concrete
You don't have to do any special trick to write a Concrete poem except to make it into a shape of your choice and it doesn't even have to rhyme.

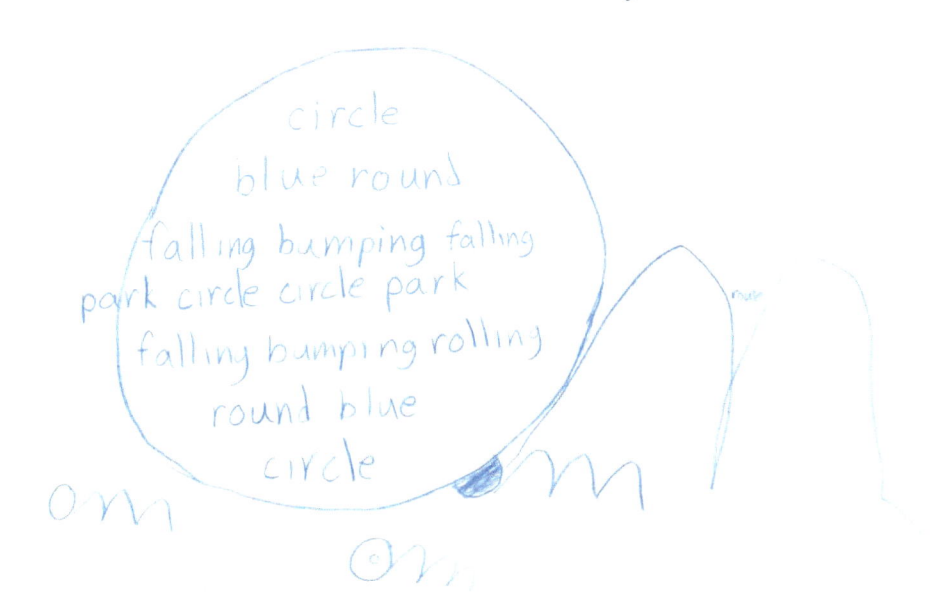

Circle

Circle
Blue Round
Rolling Bumping Falling
Park Circle Circle Park
Falling Bumping Rolling
Round Blue
Circle

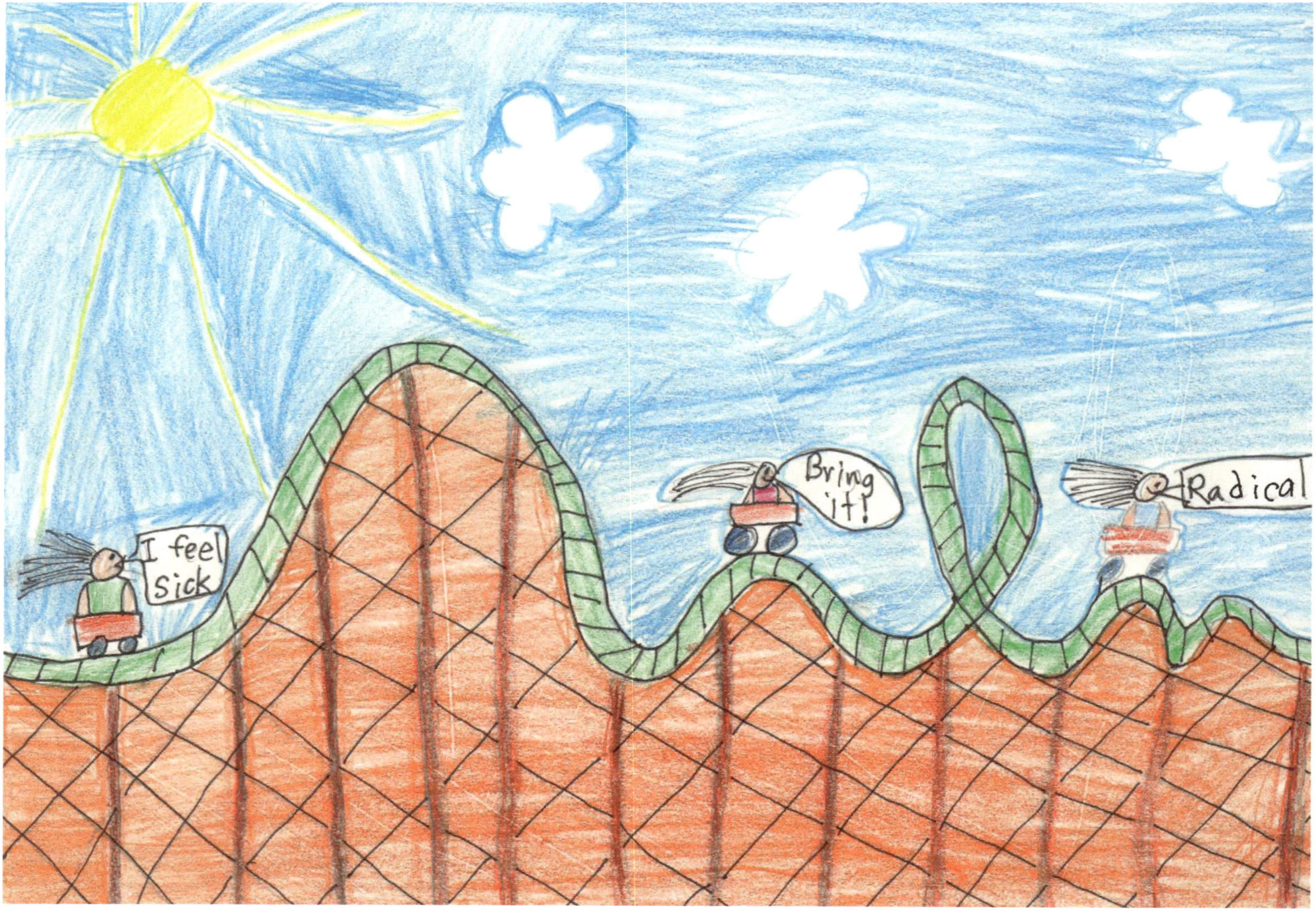
I feel sick
Bring it!
Radical

Roller Coaster

The best roller coaster in town

Goes up　　and down　　and up　　and down

Some people don't like it and I frown

up　and down　and up　and down

Chapter 4   EITHER RHYMED OR UNRHYMED POEMS – YOUR CHOICE

Persona

To write a Persona poem, you have to pretend to be the thing you are talking about. Your persona poem doesn't have to rhyme. Here is an example:

Christmas Tree

I am standing on this fake snow coated ground
Waiting for my owners to put on my elements

    Ornaments
   Garlands
    Stars
      And Strings

Oh, how I do love my specialized things!

Tennis Ball

I, a tennis ball, getting shifted from side to side
Oh, I wish that I could chide
Whoever is shifting me from side to side

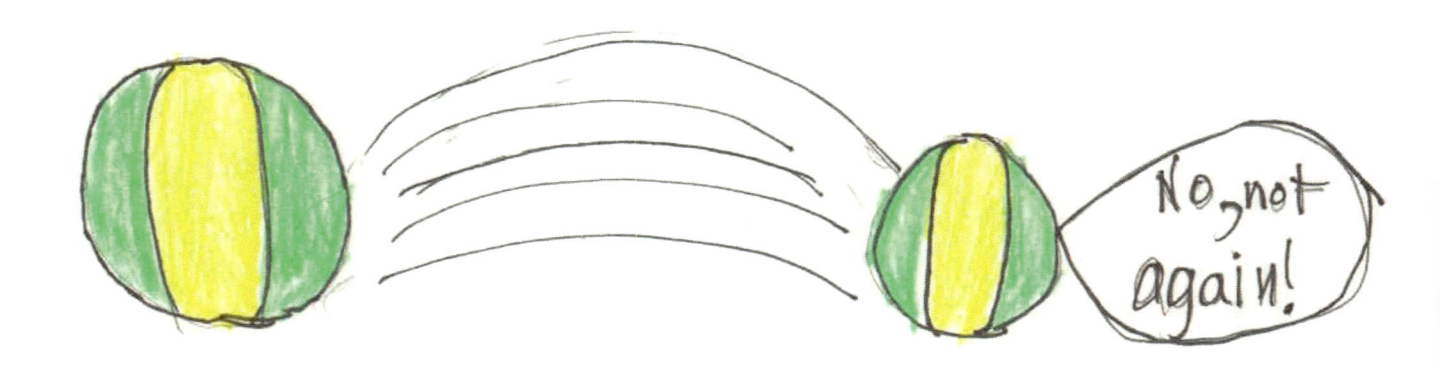

List
To write a list poem, you just write a list that doesn't have to rhyme, like the next one here:

Shopping List

Shopping List:
Bear
And Moose
Favorite Food:
Overcooked goose
Appetite:
I think I'm kinda hungry
Problem happening:
I may have some fungi
--

Chapter 5   CASSIDY INVENTION POEMS

Cassilet
This poem was invented by Cassidy Kao and its form is: a-b-a-b a-c-c a-b-a-b. It consists of 2 quatrains and 1 tercet and it goes quatrain, tercet, quatrain.

Walk

I am going on a walk
Who is coming with me
We can play and talk
Or just be plain silly

I am going on a walk
Come on let's go and play
Or we can keep our mouth in locks the whole way

I am going on a walk
Who is coming with me
We can play and talk
Or just plain silly

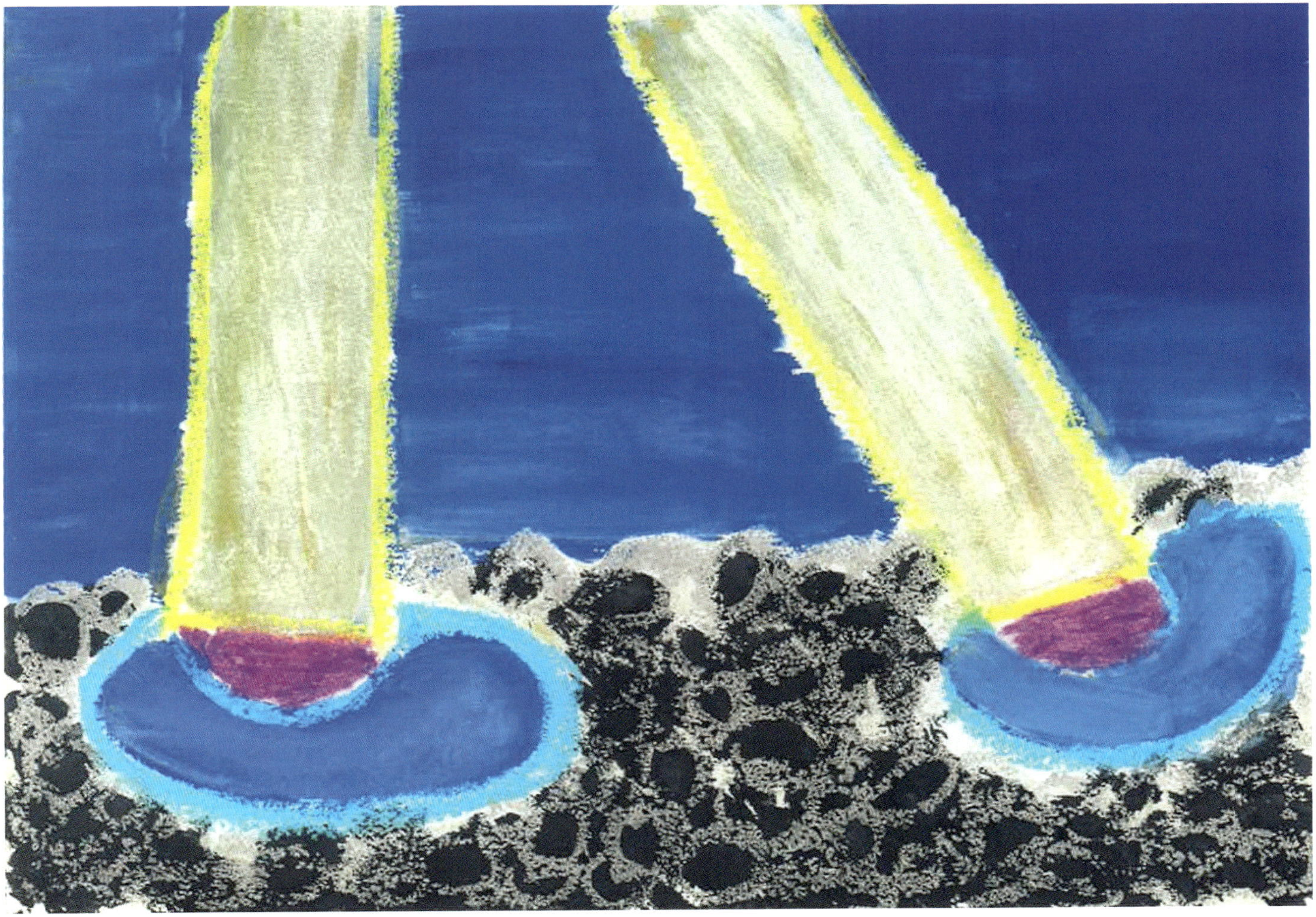

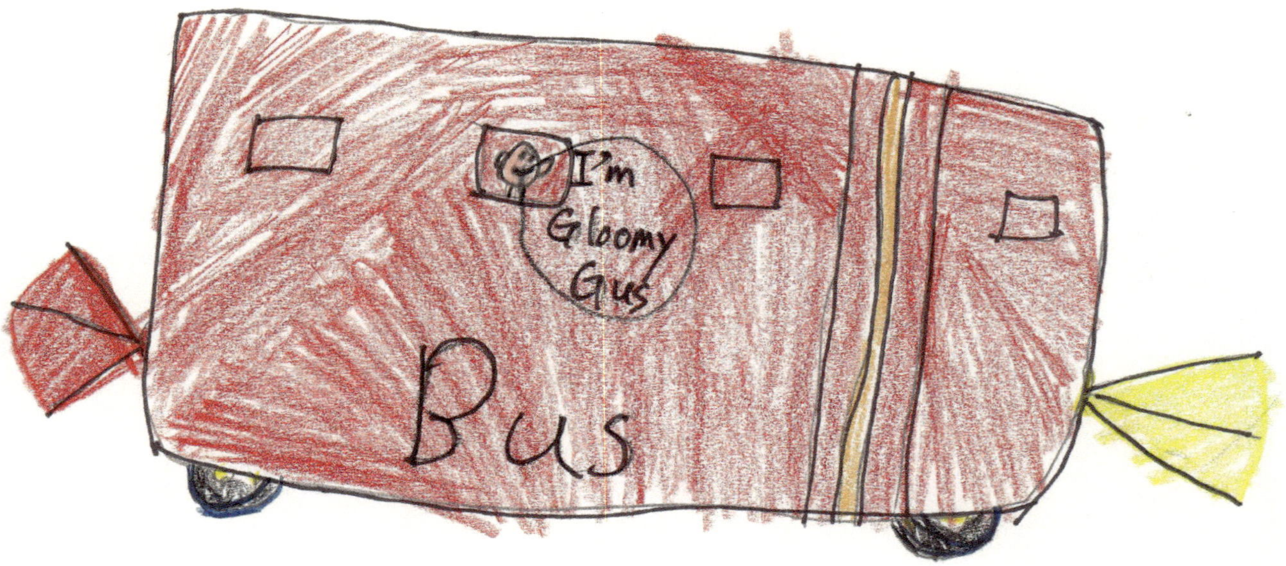
I'm
Gloomy
Gus
Bus

Freestyle
Freestyle poem can be a creation of your mind-planet (see Introduction). It can be an unrhyming poem or a rhyming poem like this one:

Bus

There once was a bus
And a man named Gloomy Gus
To sit next to his seat
Is an awesome brave feat
And though he's really neat
You never want to see him eat
Oh, and plus
He never gets off the BUS!